NFL'S GREATEST PLAYERS

WIDE RECEIVERS

By Kevin Frederickson

Kaleidoscope
Minneapolis, MN

Your Front Row Seat to the Games

This edition first published in 2020 by Kaleidoscope Publishing, Inc.

For information regarding permission, write to
Kaleidoscope Publishing, Inc.
6012 Blue Circle Drive
Minnetonka, MN 55343

Library of Congress Control Number
2019939225

ISBN
978-1-64519-078-3 (library bound)
978-1-64494-175-1 (paperback)
978-1-64519-179-7 (ebook)

Printed in the United States of America.

TABLE OF CONTENTS

CHAPTER 1

A Heady Play

Nobody expects a Super Bowl to be easy. It is a game between the two best teams in the National Football League (NFL). But the 2007 New York Giants had a historically tough test. They faced the New England Patriots. The Patriots had not lost a game all season.

FUN FACT

The 2007 Patriots were the first team in NFL history to go 16–0 in the regular season.

Very few people expected the Giants to win. But they hung tough. They were only down by four points in the fourth quarter. They needed every player to be at his best to come back. That included David Tyree. Tyree was a wide receiver. He had caught just four passes all season. But he was about to come up big.

David Tyree reaches out for a catch in Super Bowl XLII.

Giants quarterback Eli Manning faked the **handoff**. He fired a 5-yard pass over the middle. Tyree caught it. Touchdown! The Giants took the lead. But the Patriots came back to score. They got the four-point lead back. Time was running out. The Giants needed another big play. Again, they turned to Tyree.

The Giants faced third down. Only 1:15 remained on the clock. Quarterback Eli Manning dropped back. He threw the ball 32 yards toward Tyree. The pass was high. Tyree reached up. He grabbed it with two hands. He could barely hang on. So he squeezed the ball against his helmet. Tyree fell down to the ground. But he never let go of the ball.

Tyree celebrates his touchdown catch in the fourth quarter.

WHERE WIDE RECEIVERS LINE UP

The number of wide receivers and where they line up varies play to play. But they are almost always the furthest offensive players split out to the sides.

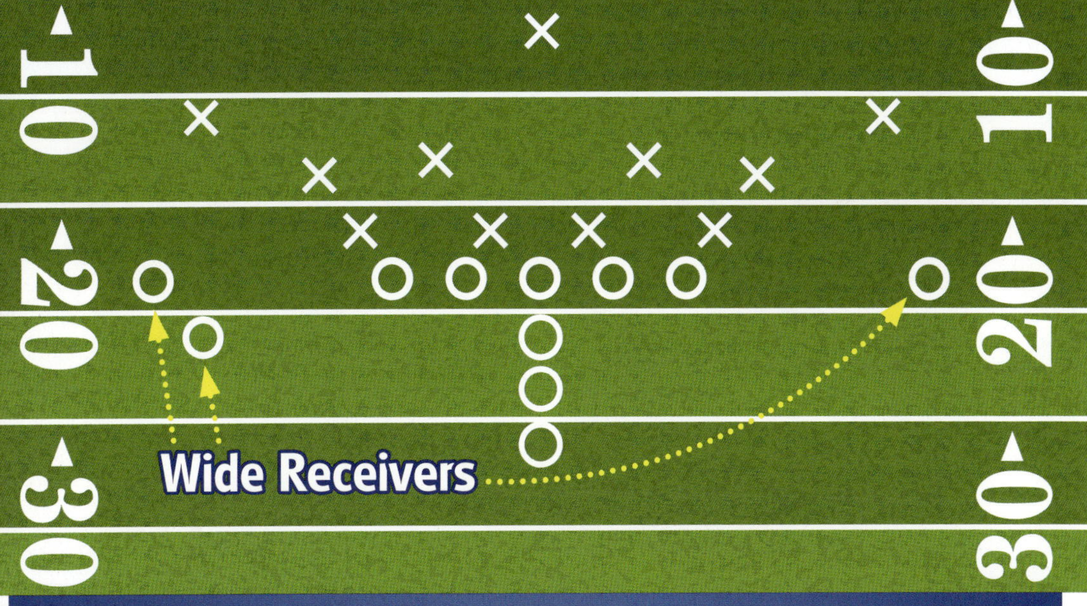

Tyree traps the ball against his helmet as Patriots safety Rodney Harrison tries to rip it away.

Tyree's play kept the drive alive. The Giants advanced to the 13-yard line. Manning passed again. He threw to the corner of the end zone. Plaxico Burress was there. He pulled the ball in. Touchdown! The Giants had the lead. Then they held on for the win.

The Patriots came into the game known for their great **offense**. Instead, it was two Giants receivers who secured the win. Tyree's catch is one of the most famous plays ever by a wide receiver. It's still talked about to this day.

Wide receivers have been key to football for many years. They come in different shapes and sizes. And the position has changed over the years. But fans have always loved their amazing catches.

CHAPTER 2

All Sizes

Terrell Owens's San Francisco 49ers were playing the Seattle Seahawks in 2002. It was *Monday Night Football.* That meant a national TV audience. And Owens wanted to put on a show. A pass headed his way in the fourth quarter. Owens jumped. So did the defender. But Owens jumped much higher. The ball landed in his hands.

He landed on his feet. Then he started running. He **tiptoed** down the sideline. A defender almost tackled him. But he was too late. Touchdown!

Owens then pulled something out of his sock. It was a black marker. Owens signed his name on the ball. Then he gave it to a fan.

Terrell Owens signs a football after scoring a touchdown on Monday Night Football.

Owens stood 6-foot-3 (1.91 m). Being tall can help receivers. They use their height to rise up for catches. Other receivers thrive in other ways. Some use speed to get open.

It was third down in Super Bowl LIII after the 2018 season. Quarterback Tom Brady knew his New England Patriots needed a big catch. And he knew just where to look. Julian Edelman was fast. He used his speed to run away from defenders. That made him really good at getting open. He became Brady's top target.

FUN FACT

Julian Edelman played quarterback in college.

TERRELL OWENS

CAREER STATS

GAMES PLAYED	219
CATCHES	1,078
RECEIVING YARDS	15,934
TOUCHDOWNS	153
YARDS PER GAME	72.8

It was early in the second half. The Patriots were on their own 14-yard line. It was third down. They did not want to have to **punt**. Brady dropped back. Edelman **sprinted** forward. He found an open space. Brady threw a quick pass. Edelman caught it for an easy first down. Then he cut to the middle of the field. He racked up even more yards.

Eight of his ten catches went for first downs. Edelman kept the Patriots moving and helped them win.

Few had heard of Edelman when he joined the Patriots. But he and Brady worked well together. Brady knew he could trust Edelman to make plays. Together, they led a strong offense.

Julian Edelman makes one of his ten catches in Super Bowl LIII.

CHAPTER 3

Jerry Rice played in the NFL until he was 42.

All-Time Greats

Jerry Rice ran left. Then he cut to the right. The play began. San Francisco 49ers quarterback Steve Young took the **snap**. Defenders paid close attention to Rice. It was no surprise. He was one of the greatest receivers ever. When playing the 49ers in the 1980s and '90s, everyone watched No. 80 closely.

Rice streaked up the field. Young spotted his star receiver. Rice was covered. Three Los Angeles Raiders defenders surrounded him. But that did not matter. Young threw. Rice soared above his defenders. He got in perfect position to catch the ball. Touchdown! And this one was special. It was his 127th. No player had scored more in a career.

Randy Moss had skills you cannot teach. He was tall. He was incredibly fast. And he could jump super high. Defenders could only hope that he dropped the ball. But that didn't happen very often.

Moss had a huge game on Thanksgiving in 2000. His Minnesota Vikings were in Dallas to play the Cowboys. In the third quarter, he streaked toward the end zone. He was almost out of space. And he was barely even looking at the ball. But he knew right where to be. The ball dropped into his hands. He dragged his feet to stay in bounds and get the touchdown.

Randy Moss uses his speed to run away from a Dallas Cowboys player on Thanksgiving Day 2000.

TIMELINE OF TOP WIDE RECEIVERS

Jerry Rice, San Francisco 49ers *(1985–2000)*, Oakland Raiders *(2001–04)*, Seattle Seahawks *(2004)*

1985

Cris Carter, Philadelphia Eagles *(1987–89)*, Minnesota Vikings *(1990–2001)*, Miami Dolphins *(2002)*

Michael Irvin, Dallas Cowboys *(1988–99)*

1990

1995

Terrell Owens, San Francisco 49ers *(1996–2003)*, Philadelphia Eagles *(2004–05)*, Dallas Cowboys *(2006–08)*, Buffalo Bills *(2009)*, Cincinnati Bengals *(2010)*

Randy Moss, Minnesota Vikings *(1998–2004, 2010)*, Oakland Raiders *(2005–06)*, New England Patriots *(2007–10)*, Tennessee Titans *(2010)*, San Francisco 49ers *(2012)*

2000

2005

Calvin Johnson, Detroit Lions *(2007–15)*

2010

Julio Jones, Atlanta Falcons *(2011–)*

DeAndre Hopkins, Houston Texans *(2013–)*

Cowboys fans knew all about great receivers. They had one for years in Michael Irvin. The Cowboys were bad when Irvin arrived. But he helped them become great. His first year was 1988. By the 1992 season, they were in the Super Bowl.

Irvin caught a touchdown pass in the second quarter. The Buffalo Bills **fumbled** on their next play. Irvin had another chance just 18 seconds later. Quarterback Troy Aikman threw his way. Irvin leaped. He caught the ball just in front of the Bills defender. Irvin was being tackled. But he reached as far as he could. It was another touchdown! The Cowboys went on to win.

FUN FACT

Michael Irvin's nickname was simply "The Playmaker."

CHAPTER 4

Julio Jones became the second Atlanta Falcons player with 10,000 receiving yards in 2018.

Who's Next?

It was late in the game. The Atlanta Falcons trailed the Dallas Cowboys. They needed a touchdown to tie. So Julio Jones went out to get one.

He ran straight down the field. A defender stayed on him tight. Finally, Jones looked up. He rose into the air. He got his hands high enough to grab the ball. The defender pushed Jones down. But Jones was already in the end zone. He tied the game with a great jumping catch.

Jones is tall at 6-foot-3 (1.91 m). He's also fast. He's one of the best in the NFL today.

FUN FACT

Jones became the fastest player to reach 10,000 career receiving yards in 2018.

DeAndre Hopkins is another tall player who is also fast. He makes jumping catches that wow fans. He has a similar style to Jones. Hopkins has quickly become a fan favorite with the Houston Texans.

JuJu Smith-Schuster is younger than Jones and Hopkins. But he also shows off his size and speed. He plays for the Pittsburgh Steelers.

RECEIVER OR RUNNING BACK?

Tarik Cohen stands to the right of his quarterback. He and his Chicago Bears are playing Miami. It is Week 6 of the 2018 season. Cohen does not wait for a handoff. He runs up the field. Bears quarterback Mitchell Trubisky hits him with a pass. Cohen takes it 50 yards for a big gain. Cohen can run the ball like a running back. But he has the speed and catching ability of a receiver. Cohen is a big part of the Bears offense.

JuJu Smith-Schuster is the youngest NFL receiver in history with 1,500 career receiving yards.

When the football game is over, Smith-Schuster is part of another game. It's *Fortnite*. Smith-Schuster plays the video game a lot in his free time. He even plays with fans. Many of today's top receivers talk with fans on the internet and social media.

During games, Michael Thomas makes a lot of catches. He gets to play with a great quarterback in Drew Brees.

Michael Thomas had more than 1,100 yards receiving in each of his first three seasons.

They play together on the New Orleans Saints. Thomas has helped the Saints be a successful offense.

Receivers come in all shapes and sizes. They all have different skills. But they are all skills that help teams win.

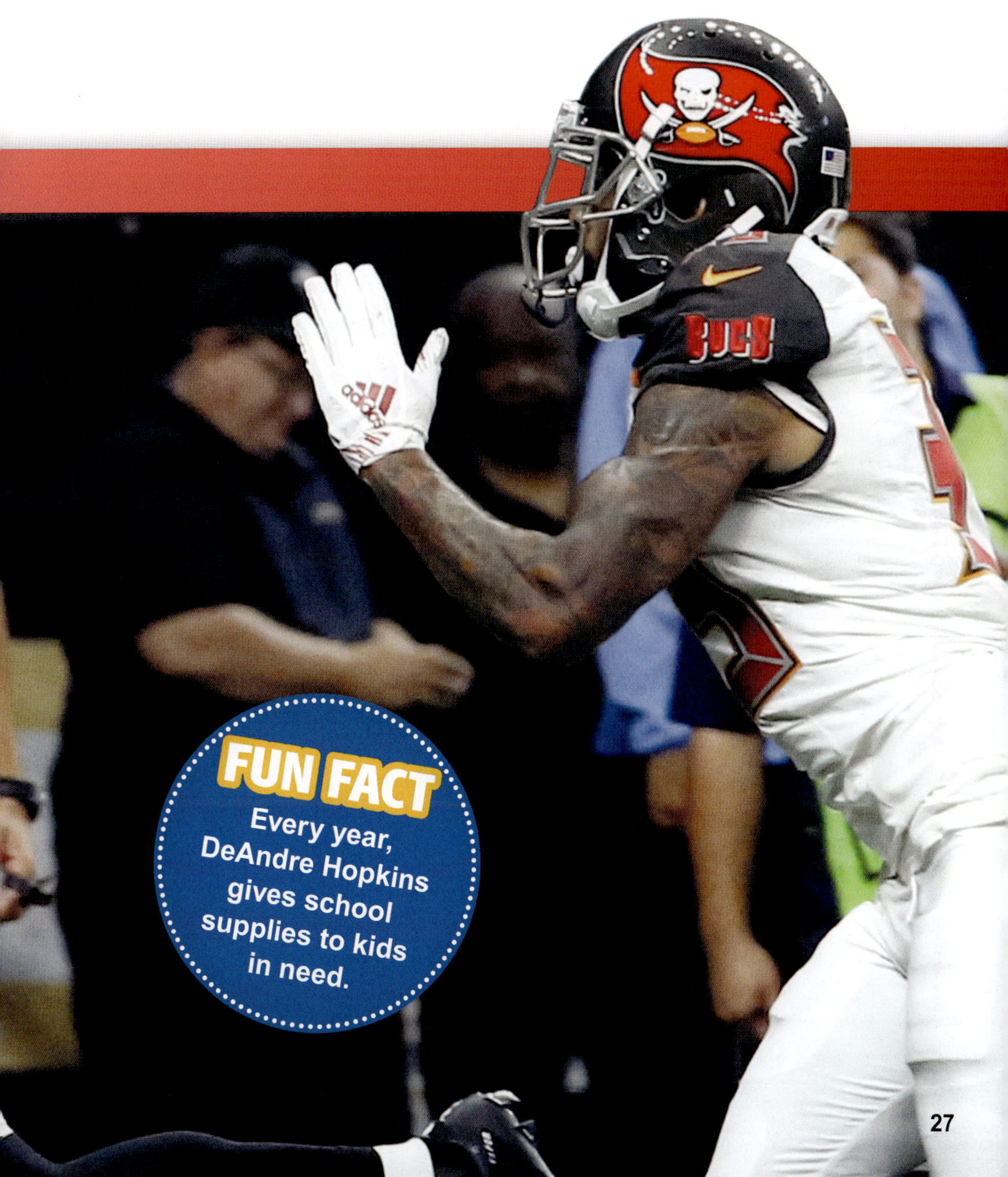

FUN FACT
Every year, DeAndre Hopkins gives school supplies to kids in need.

BEYOND THE BOOK

After reading the book, it's time to think about what you learned. Try the following exercises to jumpstart your ideas.

THINK

THAT'S NEWS TO ME. David Tyree made a big catch in the Super Bowl with the New York Giants. How might news sources be able to fill in more details about this? What new information could you find in news articles? Where could you go to find these sources?

CREATE

PRIMARY SOURCES. A primary source is an original document, photograph, or interview. Make a list of different primary sources you might be able to find about wide receivers. What new information might you learn from these sources?

SHARE

SUM IT UP. Write one paragraph summarizing the important points from this book. Make sure it's in your own words. Don't just copy what is in the text. Share the paragraph with a classmate. Does your classmate have any comments about the summary? Do they have additional questions about wide receivers?

GROW

REAL-LIFE RESEARCH. What places could you visit to learn more about wide receivers? What other information could learn while you were there?

RESEARCH NINJA

Visit www.ninjaresearcher.com/0783 to learn how to take your research skills and book report writing to the next level!

SEARCH LIKE A PRO

Learn about how to use search engines to find useful websites.

FACT OR FAKE?

Discover how you can tell a trusted website from an untrustworthy resource.

TEXT DETECTIVE

Explore how to zero in on the information you need most.

SHOW YOUR WORK

Research responsibly—learn how to cite sources.

WRITE

GET TO THE POINT

Learn how to express your main ideas.

PLAN OF ATTACK

Learn prewriting exercises and create an outline.

DOWNLOADABLE REPORT FORMS

Further Resources

BOOKS

Frederickson, Kevin. *DeAndre Hopkins*. Kaleidoscope, 2020.

Hewson, Anthony K. *Antonio Brown*. Kaleidoscope, 2020.

Levit, Joseph. *Football's G.O.A.T.* Lerner, 2019.

WEBSITES

Factsurfer.com gives you a safe, fun way to find more information.

1. Go to www.factsurfer.com.
2. Enter "Wide Receivers" into the search box and click 🔍.
3. Select your book cover to see a list of related websites.

Glossary

fumbled: When a player drops the ball, he has fumbled it. The Bills fumbled and the Cowboys recovered.

handoff: In football, a handoff happens when one player gives the ball directly to another. Mitchell Trubisky made a handoff to Tarik Cohen.

offense: The players on a team who try to score make up the offense. After the Saints defense forced a stop, Drew Brees and the offense took the field.

punt: When teams punt, they kick the ball to the other team. New England chose to punt on fourth down.

snap: The snap is what starts a play when the center gives the ball to another player. Steve Young took the snap and dropped back to pass.

sprinted: When someone has sprinted somewhere, they have run very quickly. The defender sprinted to try and catch Julian Edelman.

tiptoed: When someone has tiptoed, they have walked or run carefully using only their toes. DeAndre Hopkins tiptoed down the sidelines to stay inbounds.

Index

PHOTO CREDITS

The images in this book are reproduced through the courtesy of: Jack Dempsey/AP Images, front cover (left); Kevin Terrell/AP Images, front cover (center); Matt Patterson/AP Images, front cover (right), p. 3; EFKS/Shutterstock Images, front cover (background); Charlie Riedel/AP Images, pp. 4–5; Paul Sancya/AP Images, p. 6; Red Line Editorial, pp. 7, 13 (chart), 20 (timeline); Gene Puskar/AP Images, pp. 8–9; Rasdi Abdul Rahman/Shutterstock Images, p. 10 (marker); Lightspring/Shutterstock Images, p. 10 (football); John Froschauer/AP Images, p. 11; Paul Spinelli/AP Images, p. 12; Douglas Jones/Icon Sportswire/AP Images, p. 13 (Terrell Owens); Peter Read Miller/AP Images, pp. 14–15; Greg Trott/AP Images, pp. 16, 25; Jeff Bukowski/Shutterstock Images, pp. 17, 20 (top); Ken Wolter/Shutterstock Images, p. 18; Tim Sharp/AP Images, pp. 18–19, 21; dean bertoncelj/Shutterstock Images, pp. 20 (bottom), 30; Keith Srakocic/AP Images, pp. 22–23; Butch Dill/AP Images, pp. 26–27.

ABOUT THE AUTHOR

Kevin Frederickson is a freelance writer and editor from Ohio. He lives near Cincinnati with his golden doodle, Max.